Sea Shoes

by

Vicki Dean Mayhew

Vicki Dean Mayhew

Illustrations by Kalpart

Strategic Book Publishing and Rights Co.

Copyright © 2016 Vicki Dean Mayhew. All rights reserved.

Book Design/Layout, Illustrations and Book Cover design by Kalpart.

No part of this book may be reproduced or transmitted in any form or by any means, graphic, electronic, or mechanical, including photocopying, recording, taping, or by any information storage retrieval system, without the permission, in writing, of the publisher. For more information, send an email to support@sbpra.net, Attention: Subsidiary Rights.

Strategic Book Publishing and Rights Co., LLC
USA | Singapore
www.sbpra.com

For information about special discounts for bulk purchases,
please contact Strategic Book Publishing and Rights Co., LLC. Special Sales,
at bookorder@sbpra.net.

ISBN: 978-1-63135-014-6

Review Requested:
If you loved this book, would you please provide a review at Amazon.com?
Thank You

This book is dedicated to my Star Cousin, Erin, and her mother, my dear Aunt Marion.

I had put my dreams of writing away for good. It had been a long and frustrating journey. I shared my story with Erin who thought it was, and is magical and timeless. She told her mother, Marion, about the story. Erin came to Albuquerque to help me celebrate my 50th birthday, and had a card from Marion that said, "Don't forget about the Sea Shoes!" Enclosed was a little pair of silver shoes. Marion was at a gift shop in Sedona, Arizona, and was absolutely compelled to buy me those shoes as a gift, even without having ever read the story. I burst into tears, re-wrote the story and here we are. The world is full of a lot of magic if we are paying attention.

With much love, VDM

ONCE there was a little boy who loved his father very much, and a father who loved his little boy very much. They would go for long walks beside the sea.

One evening the wind was whispering secrets to the tall green grasses on the beach, and the sun was a giant flaming orange sphere melting into the glassy sea. The rose-colored sky stretched up to the violet clouds and the first stars of nightfall were blinking their way through the last warmth of the day.

The two walked along together and shared the magic of their dreams.

The little boy felt like walking barefoot. He liked the way the sand felt when it squeezed between his toes. He slipped his shoes off and set them on the beach. A wave rolled close and snatched the little boy's shoes away.

The little boy watched with his father for a long time as his shoes sailed away. The shoes sailed on, chasing the sun that had melted into a pool of golden light.

A starfish came upon the shoes floating across the sea. He tried them on but they didn't fit, so back into the sea they went.

"WHAT SHOES ARE THESE THAT DON'T FIT MY ARM?"
he asked the shoes in starfish talk.

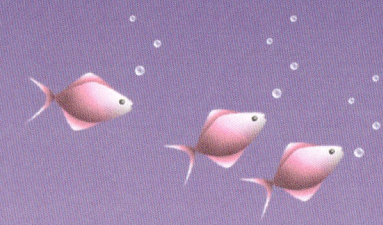

And the shoes sailed on to an emerald lagoon against the powdered sand, where palm trees bow their heads to the sea breezes below a clear blue sky, to a place where sandcastle dreams land . . . but the shoes sailed on.

A family of dolphins found the shoes. They tossed them back and forth, ringing them around their noses, and stealing them away from each other as they chased their tails through the waves.

"WHAT SHOES ARE THESE THAT DON'T FIT MY FIN?" they asked each other in dolphin talk, and back into the sea they went.

The shoes sailed on.

They sailed into the starry night, when the charcoal clouds circled down to the gray-green sea, and lightning flashed. The sea rose and fell, and angry curls broke out of the depths of the darkened sea.

An octopus drifted close and reached out with one long arm, pulling the shoes toward her, looking for a tasty meal. But it wasn't dinner and they didn't fit on her long arm either.

"WHAT SHOES ARE THESE THAT DON'T FIT MY ARM?" she asked the shoes in octopus talk, and back into the sea they went.

The shoes sailed on toward a shipping lane and an ocean-liner so big it blocked out the sky, forcing the sea shoes out of her path. Engines churned, music blared, people laughed, dolphins danced in the waves left behind, and the shoes sailed on.

They sailed toward a rocky shore with the full moon shining so bright the rocks were giant gemstones glowing beneath the waves.

A walrus scooped the sea shoes up and tickled them with his mighty whiskers. He looked at them closely, poking at them with his long ivory tusk. He tried to slip them over the end of the smooth tooth.

"WHAT SHOES ARE THESE THAT WON'T FIT MY TUSK?" he asked himself in walrus talk. Since they didn't fit him either, they slipped right off, into the sea, and the shoes sailed on.

The ocean grew colder, and crystal mountains of ice drifted near. The sky was brilliant with rainbows of northern lights shimmering into snowflakes, dancing down, down, down to the pitch black sea.

A polar bear mom plucked the shoes from the sea and, with one giant paw, tossed them to her cubs. They sniffed and snorted and nudged them with their cold charcoal noses. Growling and grizzling, they played and fought over the shoes, tossing them back and forth and catching them on one toe.

"WHAT SHOES ARE THESE THAT DON'T FIT MY PAW?" they asked each other in polar bear talk.

But they wouldn't even fit on one toe, so when the cubs tired of playing with the shoes, they tossed them back to the sea.

And the shoes sailed on to the quiet sea with the father and mother whales singing whale songs to their children and slapping their colossal tails into circles of waves around the sea shoes.

They sang:

> *"In the twilight of the evening,*
> *This sweet story came to me;*
> *And I sing it to my children,*
> *Little shoes that went to sea.*

And the ocean's full of mystery,
Silent moonbeams fill the sky;
Little shoes begin their journey,
Little boy, he waves good-bye.

And the ocean tossed the sea shoes,
Dolphins dancing in the night;
Trying to ring them on their noses,
Singing songs in the moonlight.

Wishful whale who tried the shoes on,
Polar bear, not meant for you;
Octopus and silly starfish,
They don't fit, you know it's true.

In the twilight of the evening,
This sweet story came to me;
And I sing it to my children,
Little shoes that went to sea.

Walrus whispers to the wind,
And double rainbows fill the sky;
So much beauty in this journey,
All the animals did try.

Sandcastle dreams are landing there,
Rose-colored sky is yawning;
Shimmering stars that fade away,
Another day is dawning.

Misty mornings, singing seagulls,
Feel the magic in the air;
Little shoes the journey's over,
Wave comes close and leaves them there.

In the twilight of the evening,
This sweet story came to me;
And I sing it to my children,
Little shoes that went to sea."

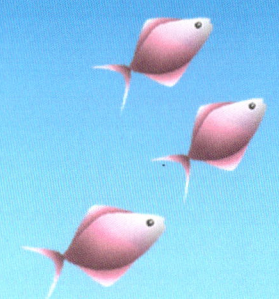

A double rainbow appeared on the distant horizon, calling to the sea shoes. The shoes sailed on.

The years passed, and many other animals found those shoes and tried them on,

but not one time did they ever fit.

Then, one day, there was a father who loved his little boy very much, and a little boy who loved his father very much. The father took long walks beside the sea with his son, like his father did with him when he was small, and they shared their dreams.

One misty morning the seagulls were calling and announcing the beginning of another new day. The crimson sky was saying goodnight to the falling stars. The warm, golden light from the sun was filtering across the shore. The soft sea breeze whispered of magic to the tall green grasses bowing their heads.

A wave came close and set the sea shoes on the beach. The little boy found them and tried them on. Delighted that they fit, from then on he wore them for every walk on the beach with his dad.

CPSIA information can be obtained at www.ICGtesting.com
Printed in the USA
LVIW01n2353130417
530800LV00002B/6